Disney · PIXAR

COCO

MIGUEL AND THE AMAZING ALEBRIJES

By Roni Capin Rivera-Ashford and Aarón Rivera-Ashford
Illustrated by Ricardo De Los Angeles

A Random House PICTUREBACK® Book
Random House 🏠 New York

Copyright © 2017 Disney Enterprises, Inc. and Pixar. All rights reserved. Published in the United States by Random House Children's Books, a division of Penguin Random House LLC, 1745 Broadway, New York, NY 10019, and in Canada by Penguin Random House Canada Limited, Toronto, in conjunction with Disney Enterprises, Inc. Pictureback, Random House, and the Random House colophon are registered trademarks of Penguin Random House LLC.

randomhousekids.com

ISBN 978-0-7364-3766-0

Printed in the United States of America

10 9 8 7 6 5 4 3 2 1

Miguel Rivera was excited to go to school. His teacher had promised to tell the kids about a **special project** they were going to make. He could hardly wait!

"Good morning, class," said Señora Sena, Miguel's teacher. "Today we will be doing a papier-mâché project!"

Miguel was thrilled. "Oh, yay! We're going to make piñatas."

"No, not piñatas," she said. "For our special project, we'll be making . . .

". . . alebrijes!"

"Ale-what?" one of the students asked.

"Alebrijes—they're colorful sculptures of fantastical creatures," said Señora Sena. "Alebrijes were invented about one hundred years ago. They are a combination of ancient and modern Mexican art forms."

"How did they get that name?" Miguel asked.

"The word *alebrije* came to an artist in a dream," his teacher answered. "That's why there is **something magical** about them."

"To start the project, you must be inspired," Señora Sena said. "Your inspiration will come from animals that live here in Santa Cecilia. Go exploring, and make a list of eight of your favorite animals."

"Eight?" Miguel said. **"That's a lot!"**

"You don't have to make eight alebrijes, Miguel. It's okay to make just a few, or even one. And the sculptures can be of a particular animal or a combination. Making a list of animals will inspire you to use your imagination."

Now that Miguel understood, he was excited to get started. After school, he went to his favorite place, Mariachi Plaza, to look for animals.

Right away, he saw pigeons gathered around a fountain. "Oh, this is going to be so easy," said Miguel. "Pigeon: animal número uno."

Out of the corner of his eye, Miguel spotted a lizard scurrying past. He tried to catch it, but it was too fast. **"Lizard: animal número dos,"** he said.

As a band warmed up, the sound of their music caught Miguel's attention.

"It's Armando and His Acoustic Armadillos," he said. "They are a fantástico group! **Armadillo: animal número tres.**"

¡ARMANDO Y SUS ARMADILLOS ACÚSTICOS!

Miguel searched the plaza, but he didn't see any more animals.

"Maybe this is going to be harder than I thought," he said.
He sat for a moment, then decided to head home to ask Abuelita for help.

When Miguel got home, he told his grandmother about his class project.

"Abuelita, we're making alebrijes in school, and I need to find five more animals to inspire me. Can you help?"

Abuelita was excited. "Ooh, I love alebrijes. They are as unique as their creators. I'm sure you'll make something beautiful. ¡Vamos! Let's find inspiration from **our familia**."

Abuelita pulled out old pictures of the Rivera family
that they used every year on **Día de los Muertos**,
the Day of the Dead, for the ofrenda—the family altar.

One of the photos showed Mamá Imelda with a gray cat. "Your great-great-grandmother Imelda loved that cat. She named her **Pepita**," said Abuelita.

"Thank you, Abuelita. **Cat: animal número cuatro.**"

"Do you have a favorite animal?" Miguel asked.

Abuelita laughed. "Yes. I once had a pet goat named Diego. Did you know goats will eat just about anything? He would even eat our laundry."

Miguel laughed. "Goat: animal número cinco!"

"What about you, Mamá Coco?" Miguel asked. His great-grandmother had been listening to them all along.

"Bonita," she whispered, pointing out the window.

Miguel turned and saw a red-tailed hawk in the sky. "Wow, I never would have noticed that! Hawk: animal número seis," he said. "Gracias, Mamá Coco."

Just then, a butterfly landed on the windowsill. Abuelita leaned over and whispered to Miguel, "In our country, butterflies, or mariposas, are known as animal guides. And you know what, mijito? It is said that with their migration to Mexico every year, they **bring lost spirits home** for Día de los Muertos."

"That's so cool, Abuelita," Miguel said. **"Butterfly: animal número siete.** Only one more to go!"

Miguel searched everywhere for one last animal to put on his list. He walked to a quiet area just outside of town.

"Music is meant to bring people together," he said as he began to play his homemade guitar. "Maybe it will help me find my last animal, too."

Suddenly, he heard a noise. It was his perro pal, Dante, singing along. "How could I forget about you, Dante? Dog: animal número ocho!"

In school the next day, Miguel
worked hard on his project.
   "You've got some interesting
combinations," said his teacher.
"How did you choose your alebrijes?"
   "I don't feel like I chose
them, Señora Sena. In a
magical way, it feels
like **they chose me.**"

At home, Miguel presented his familia with the alebrijes. First, he gave Mamá Coco one that resembled the hawk she had spotted.

Next, he gave Abuelita one of Diego with a piece of her favorite apron hanging from his mouth. She laughed so hard. She loved it!

Finally, Miguel placed the alebrijes of Pepita and Dante next to the ofrenda. He was proud of his creations. Miguel knew in his heart that Mamá Imelda would have loved hers. And he also had a feeling she would like Pepita's **new friend**, Dante.